written by
Deborah Underwood

Good Night, Baddies

illustrated by
Juli Kangas

Beach Lane Books • New York London Toronto Sydney New Delhi

For the baddies in all of us—D. U.

For Judy Sue—J. K.

BEACH LANE BOOKS • An imprint of Simon & Schuster Children's Publishing Division • 1230 Avenue of the Americas, New York, New York 10020 • Text copyright © 2016 by Deborah Underwood • Illustrations copyright © 2016 by Juli Kangas • All rights reserved, including the right of reproduction in whole or in part in any form. • BEACH LANE BOOKS is a trademark of Simon & Schuster, Inc. • For information about special discounts for bulk purchases, please contact Simon & Schuster Special Sales at 1-866-506-1949 or business@simonandschuster.com. • The Simon & Schuster Speakers Bureau can bring authors to your live event. For more information or to book an event, contact the Simon & Schuster Speakers Bureau at 1-866-248-3049 or visit our website at www.simonspeakers.com. • Book design by Lauren Rille • The text for this book is set in Caslon Antique. • The illustrations for this book are rendered in watercolor with oil washes over the top. • Manufactured in China • 0216 SCP • First Edition • 10 9 8 7 6 5 4 3 2 1 • Library of Congress Cataloging-in-Publication Data • Names: Underwood, Deborah, author. | Kangas, Juli, illustrator. • Title: Good night, baddies / Deborah Underwood ; illustrated by Juli Kangas. • Description: New York : Beach Lane Books, [2016] | Summary: "After a full day of evil schemes, fairy tale baddies return home to spend time with their friends and get ready for bed in this cozy bedtime book"—Provided by publisher. • Identifiers: LCCN 2015033100 | ISBN 978-1-4814-0984-1 (hardback) | ISBN 978-1-4814-0986-5 (eBooks) • Subjects: | CYAC: Bedtime—Fiction. | Villains—Fiction. | Fairy tales. • BISAC: JUVENILE FICTION / Bedtime & Dreams. | JUVENILE FICTION / Humorous Stories. | JUVENILE FICTION / Monsters. • Classification: LCC PZ7.U4193 Go 2016 | DDC [E]—dc23 LC record available at http://lccn.loc.gov/2015033100

Sun dips down; the day has gone.
Witches, wolves, and giants yawn.
Queen and dragon, troll and gnome:
tired baddies head for home.

Baddie buddies meet each other,
share their news and greet each other.
"Did you get your treasure back?"
"Did you catch that awful Jack?"

Baddies sit politely dining,
no one throwing food or whining.
All day long they must be vile;
now, at night, they chat and smile.

Evil queen, take off your crown;
trade pajamas for your gown.

Tuck your poisoned fruit away.
Find Snow White another day.

Poor old troll, your life is tough:
a muddy wait for three goats gruff.
You deserve a nice long scrub,
so add some bubbles to the tub.

Wolves, today was not so good.
You didn't catch Red Riding Hood.
You huffed and puffed without success.
But brush your fangs, please, nonetheless.

Rumpelstiltskin wants a story,
one that's sweet, not grim or gory.
Dragon, a refreshing drink
will quench your fire, don't you think?

Bedtime now, but Giant's scared.
Helpful witches come prepared.
Underneath the bed they peer—
nope, no princess hiding here!

Baddies turn to sleepyheads,
tuck each other into beds.

Warm and cozy, snuggled tight,
baddies read by candlelight.

Underneath a starry sky,
sing a baddie lullaby.
Day will bring more evil schemes.
Good night, baddies . . .